WALT DISNEY'S

ALICE IN WONDERLAND

Published in 2006 by Dalmatian Press, LLC.

PRINTED IN CHINA

06 07 08 GUA 5 4 3 2 1

One lovely hazy, lazy summer's afternoon little Alice was busy making a daisy chain, as she perched on the limb of a big oak tree while, below her, her elder sister read from a dull old history book.

"Look, Dinah!" whispered the little girl, as she twisted the daisy chain into a crown and popped it on the kitten's head. "Now you're a Kitty Queen."

"Mee-ow!" Dinah clawed at the crown. It slipped from her head and fluttered down on to the bonnet of Alice's prim sister.

"Alice!" said the history-reader severely. "Please pay attention!"

Suddenly, however, the little girl decided that she was tired of listening to history. And, taking the kitten, she slipped from the tree without her sister seeing, tiptoed away and finally flung herself among the flowers.

It was lovely there and her thoughts went wandering. She imagined that Dinah could talk, that rabbits lived in little houses and that flowers could play music and was just imagining a lot of other things when she slipped softly into Slumberland.

Dinah was the first to see the White Rabbit and to note that he wore a waistcoat, held a watch in his hand, and kept crying: "Oh, my fur and whiskers! I'm late! I'm SO late!"

"Mee-ow! Mee-ow!" mewed the kitten, trying to make Alice notice this astonishing thing.

"Stop making that silly noise," laughed Alice, looking at the hurrying rabbit. "It's only a rabbit with a waistcoat and a——" she stopped and jumped to her feet.

"That *is* curious," she went on. "Why has he a watch? What could he possibly be late for?" And Alice ran after the White Rabbit calling:

"Mr. Rabbit! Wait, wait for me!"

"No, no, no, I'm overdue!" called out the creature, and he ducked into a hole in the base of a tree.

Before she knew what she was doing, Alice followed the rabbit and THEN it happened. The floor slanted downward, Alice slipped and then she was falling—FALLING headlong down a deep, deep shaft.

"Good-bye, Dinah!" she called out. "Good-bye-e-e-e!"

At first the little girl fell swiftly but, as her skirt acted like a parachute, she slowed down and landed very gently on the bottom of the shaft.

"Hi!" she shouted, seeing the White Rabbit vanish through a door. "Wait——" But Alice found the door was much too tiny for her to go through. All the same for that, she seized the Doorknob and shook it.

"Ouch!" wailed the Doorknob. "That hurts!"

"I—I b-beg your pardon!" The little girl let go of the Doorknob as if it had been red hot.

"You did give me a turn."

The Doorknob wriggled his nose back into shape. "You gave ME a turn, you mean!" he said. Then he smiled. "But as one good turn deserves another, what can I do for you?"

"I'm looking for a rabbit," explained Alice, "so may I look through your keyhole?"

"With pleasure," came the Doorknob's reply, as he yawned. "Ho hummmm! There you are!"

"Yes, there it is," cried the little girl, peering through the keyhole. "Oh, I simply *must* get through."

The Doorknob laughed. "Sorry, you're much too big." He looked over the little girl's head. "Why not try that bottle?" he added.

Alice spun round. "What bottle?" she asked.

"Bottle?" grunted the Doorknob. "Why, the one on the table, of course." And, to the visitor's amazement, a table appeared with a little bottle on it.

"Hmmm!" murmured Alice doubtfully, as she took up the bottle and saw that it had a label on it with the two words: "DRINK ME!"

"Go on, my dear," said the Doorknob. "Drink heartily. You'll like that stuff!"

Alice *did* like it. It tasted like cherry tart, pineapple and strawberries all rolled into one. "It's lov——" she began, when she suddenly shrank until she was so small that she couldn't hold on to the bottle. "Ooooh!" she wailed as she and the bottle fell over. "Where am I? Oh, dear, am I here at all?" And she was almost invisible under the label marked: "DRINK ME!"

"Of course you're there," cried the Doorknob, "and what is more, you would be the right size to pass through my door if it wasn't locked."

"*Locked?*" wailed Alice.

"That's right—locked!" laughed the Doorknob. "But you need not worry, because you've got the key, so that's all right, isn't it?"

"Key?" echoed the girl. "What key?"

"Goodness gracious," teased the Doorknob, wriggling his fat nose with bubbly laughter. "Don't tell me that you've left the key—tee-hee—up THERE!" And he nodded toward the table that now towered over Alice's head. "Well, well, what *will* you do next?"

Almost crying with disappointment, the girl looked up and saw a key appear on the table. "Oh, *bother!*" she muttered. "How can I get it?" And she hugged a leg of the table, managed to climb about two and a quarter inches, and then slid down again onto the floor. "Whatever shall I do? Can't you tell me, Mr. Doorknob?"

"Do?" echoed that fellow. "Why, try the box, naturally. That seems the sensible thing to do."

"What b——?" began Alice, when a tiny box appeared at her feet. Really it was most astonishing how things appeared just when she wanted them most. "Oh!" she gasped as she opened it. "What a sweet little sweet!" And she took out a heart-shaped sweet with the words "EAT ME!" printed on it. "Well, here goes!" And she popped it into her mouth.

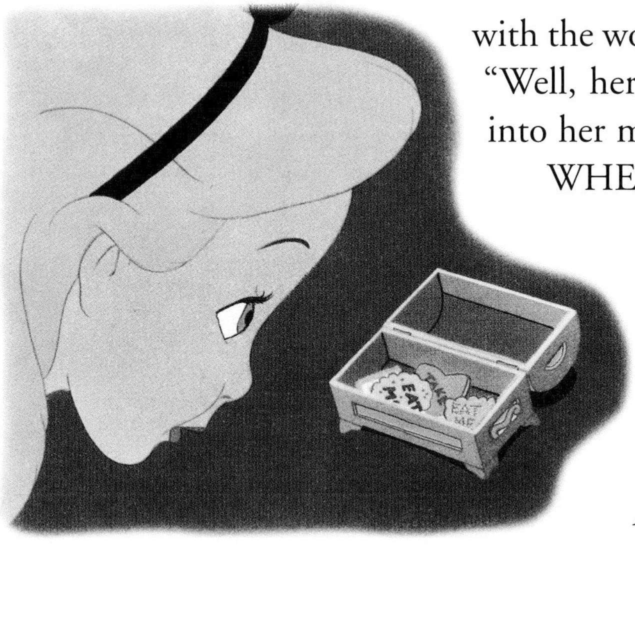

WHEEEEEEE!

Up she shot like a rocket, in all directions, so that one of her feet pressed against the Doorknob and her head against the ceiling. "Boo-hoo!" sobbed poor Alice. "What shall I do?"

And great salt tears splashed from her eyes to the floor in such a stream that the little room was soon half filled with saltwater.

"Stop crying," gurgled the Doorknob, as water washed over him. "You'll d-drown me, young lady. Quickly! Grab the bottle. The BOTTLE! *Look!*" And he pointed with the tip of his nose showing above the water.

The girl's huge hand seized the bottle and she gulped down the rest of the MAKE-U-SMALL fluid.

In a flash she was so tiny that she fell—plonk—right into the bottle and floated away on the waves made by her own tears.

"Have a—gurgle—good trip!" called out the Doorknob as Alice-in-the-bottle drifted through his keyhole into the black darkness beyond that door.

"Deary, deary me!" she murmured. "I'll never cry so much again. Never!"

"Never, never, never..." echoed a voice, singing in what Alice now knew to be a dense fog. "Do a thing about the weather," went on the singer, "for the weather never ever does a thing for me. Ho, Ho! A sailor's life is the life for me." The voice stopped its singing. "Ahoy there, Dodo!" it cried. "Where away, Dodo?"

"Dodo?" the girl in the bottle asked herself. "But there *are* no Dodoeseseses left anywhere." But, all the same for that, she called out in despair, "Dodo! Mister Dodo, do something to help me. Please, Dodo, don't go!"

Unluckily she couldn't be heard above the shouting of that invisible Dodo.

"Three points to starboard, me hearties," it cried. "Pull away, there! Pull away! Heave *ho*! HEAVE HO!"

Suddenly the fog lifted and Alice saw the strangest sight of all, for there was a Dodo riding on a Toucan's beak and being pushed along by an Eaglet. Yes, and the girl also saw other odd creatures doing odd things: a Pelican propelling a Parrot, and an Owl on a log.

"Help!" squeaked Alice. "Would you mind helping me?"

No one took the slightest notice of her. Lobsters paddled by, mice cut through the water, and in the distance was none other than the White Rabbit using an upturned umbrella like a boat.

Suddenly the worst happened: in her eagerness to reach help, the little girl spilled herself through the neck of the bottle and only just escaped being drowned by being washed up onto an island where the Dodo, the Toucan, the Eaglet, the Pelican, the Owl and the rest were running round and *round* and ROUND in a circle.

"Come on!" called the Dodo. "Join the Caucus Race. Keep running. Finest way I know to get dry. Go on, off you go!"

Alice kept up that race as long as she could but, suddenly spotting the White Rabbit, she broke free and dashed after it. "Stop!" she shouted. "White RABBIT! Please stop!" The rabbit gave her one look, hoisted his umbrella, to drench himself with the water it held, shook himself like a dog and vanished into a small wood. Away went the little girl after the White Rabbit, but he was nowhere to be seen.

"Puff—pant—gasp!" she panted, as she sat on a hollow log of wood.

"Where *did* that rabbit go? He's as slippery as an eel. I can't——" She stopped and stared at two strange figures standing by the log, one labeled "TWEEDLEDEE" and the other, exactly like him, "TWEEDLEDUM."

Alice curtsied in the most ladylike manner.

"How do you do?" she said. "My name is Alice and I'm following a White Rabbit. I really *must* go. Good-bye! "

"Beep!" cried Tweedledum. "You can't go yet."

"Boop!" added Tweedledee. "Not until we've told you the story of *The Walrus and the Carpenter*, or *The Story of the Curious Oysters*. You're a curious child, so here is a curious story. Listen. Boop!"

"Yes, listen. Beep!" cried Tweedledum.

So, being a *very* curious person, Alice listened to the tale the two twins had to tell.

• • • • •

Once upon a long time ago (chorused Tweedledum and Tweedledee) on a fine summer's day in the middle of the night the Walrus and the Carpenter strolled from the moon shadows into the sunlight on a wide beach by the side of a lonely ocean.

It was so full of sand that the Carpenter was almost buried in the sand he emptied from his shoe. "Idea!" exclaimed that fellow, tapping his head with his hammer to show where the idea was coming from. "Let us sweep away this sand."

Then the Walrus used the hammer as a lever, flipped the Carpenter out of the sand and sent him—uggle, wubble, bubble—into the water.

"Oysters!" cried the Carpenter, raising his head from the water.

"Out of my way," said the Walrus pompously. "I'll deal with this."

And, would you believe it, he persuaded the little oysters to take no notice of their mother's warning but follow him and the Carpenter out of the water.

"We'll have a lovely feed!" he declared. "Quickly, Carpenter, build a restaurant."

The Carpenter worked swiftly, found some drift-wood and built a restaurant.

"Good!" cried the Walrus. "Now, Carpenter, you go into the kitchen and get bread, salt, pepper, vinegar and water. I'll look after the oysters."

And he *did* look after those poor little oysters. He gobbled them all up and had just finished when in came the Carpenter with a loaded tray.

"Pig!" he yelled when he saw what had happened; and the story ends as the angry Carpenter chased the Walrus down the wide, wide beach, waving his hammer.

• • • • •

"Oh!" cried Alice, when the tale was told. "What a sad story." And she started to leave.

"Wait!" chorused Tweedledum and Tweedledee. "Now we will recite to you. The recitation is called 'Father William' and we know you will like it." But, as they cleared their throats, Alice waved good-bye and dashed away through the trees.

The little girl did her best to forget the story she had just heard as she plunged through the wood looking for the White Rabbit. Suddenly she came to a clearing and stared at a little house with a thatched roof.

"Ah!" she exclaimed. "I wonder who lives there?"

As if in answer to her question, a window flew open and out popped the White Rabbit's head.

"Mary Ann!" he shouted. "Oh, bother the girl. Where could she have put my gloves?"

"Rabbit! White Rabbit!" called out a delighted Alice. "I am glad I've found you at last. I've been chasing you for ages and ages. Do tell me——?"

She stopped speaking as the White Rabbit came dashing out of the front door, his watch still in his hand and a little trumpet in the other hand.

"You tell ME!" he shrilled. "Where are my gloves? Come, Mary Ann, where did you put my gloves?"

"But I—that is I'm not… you see I've been trying to… Oh, dear, *do* tell me why you are in such a hurry!" The little girl hardly knew what she was saying she was so confused by the impatient rabbit.

"Go, go, go!" the creature shrilled, pointing to the door. "Fetch my gloves at once, Mary Ann. My gloves! At once! Do you hear? Off with you!" And the White Rabbit pushed Alice rudely toward the door. "I'm late enough already, I'll have you know, and now you're making me later still."

"Yes, but what are you late *for*?" cried Alice. "And I'm NOT Mary Ann. My name is——"

"Mary Ann!" snapped the White Rabbit. "That's why you must fetch my gloves. Off with you! Shoo!"

"My goodness," muttered the little girl to herself, as she walked into the thatched cottage. "I'll be taking orders from Dinah next." And she marched up the staircase of the cottage wondering why she hadn't told the White Rabbit to find the real Mary Ann, or find his own gloves. She reached a bedroom and began to rummage about. "Hmm! I wonder where a rabbit *would* keep his gloves. In here?" She giggled as she lifted the lid from a jar of biscuits. "Well, no, perhaps not!" She peered closely at a biscuit and saw that it was labeled: "TAKE ONE."

"That *is* an idea," she told herself. And she did!

Oh, dear! oh, dear! The same thing happened as had happened before. The moment Alice began to eat the biscuit, as she had eaten the sweet, she commenced to grow at an alarming rate. Her head hit the ceiling, she was obliged to put her arms through the windows, and one foot pushed the White Rabbit down the stairs, as he came in to see what was keeping her, while the other crashed through a greenhouse with a tinkle-winkle-inkle of glass.

Biff! Bump! Bonk!

The White Rabbit rolled through the wrecked front door, picked himself up, looked up at the thatched cottage, blew his little trumpet and yelled at the top of his voice:

"HELP! MONSTER! HELP! ASSISTANCE!"

"Stop talking nonsense!" cried Alice, as she tried to scratch her head, but only managed to scratch the thatch instead. "I'm not a monster. I'm Alice."

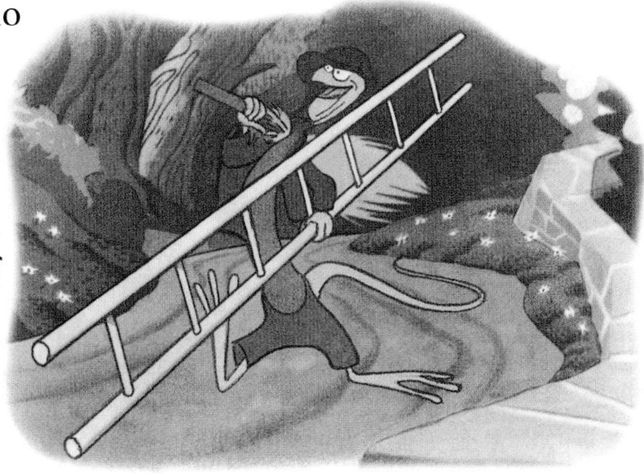

The White Rabbit took no notice of her, however, but seeing the Dodo approaching dashed up to him. "Look!" he yelled. "A Monster, Dodo, in my house. Oh, my poor roof and rafters. Oh, my poor windows and walls. Something must be done."

"Indeed—yes!" cried the Dodo. "Ah! I have it!" And he pointed to where Bill, the chimney-sweep lizard, was steaming up with his ladder. "Bill!" he roared. "Do your duty. Pull that Monster up through the chimney. No!" he went on as Bill climbed up his ladder but was so frightened he came down again quicker than he had gone up. "I have a better idea. We'll BURN the Monster out.

Don't worry, Rabbit, I'll soon have the house clear of Monsters. Leave everything to me—Dodo! I'm the fellow to *do* things."

In vain the White Rabbit squeaked his protests, the Dodo started to bring out the furniture and to break it up for firewood. He got a wheelbarrow from somewhere and whistled happily as he worked.

"There!" he cried at last, rubbing his hands together. "Now for a light. Have you a match, Rabbit?"

Before he knew what he was doing, the stupid White Rabbit had handed over a match and the smoke began to rise.

"Oh! Oh, dear!" wailed Alice, as she saw the smoke. "This is getting serious. White Rabbit! White Rabbit! How stupid you are. You may get rid of me but you'll get rid of your house and furniture at the same time."

Suddenly Alice had an idea. "I've got it," she cried. "If I eat something else I might grow small again." And she looked round for something she *could* eat. "Carrots!" she shouted gleefully, as she saw the vegetable garden.

Snatching up a carrot, Alice began to munch it. At the second bite she shrank and shrank and shrank until she was smaller than she had ever been before. "Help!" she shrilled. "Oh, dear, when *will* I become the correct size again? White Rabbit, where are you?"

Alice dashed out of the cottage and saw the rabbit running away.

"Can't stop!" cried the creature. "I'm so terribly late."

Alice chased the White Rabbit into a flower garden, scattering the butterflies. "Wait!" she cried. "Please wait just a teeny-weeny minute." Then she stopped to examine some curious butterflies.

"How curious they are!" she said.

"Not really," said a Red Rose. "They are bread-and-butterflies, that's all.

"I beg your pardon," gasped the little girl, as she stared at the rose. "But—but did you s-speak?"

"Of course I did!" cried the rose. "Why not?"

"But flowers *can't* speak!" protested Alice.

"Who said so?" demanded an Iris. "We can speak all right, if there's anyone worth talking to." And she studied the tiny Alice through her lorgnette.

"We sing, too!" put in some Pansies.

"That is correct," said Red Rose solemnly. "Sssh!" She tapped her baton. "Now, girls, we shall sing 'Golden Afternoon'. Sound your A, Lily."

Then the flowers began to sing:

"Little bread-and-butterflies,
Kiss the tulips
And the sun is like a toy balloon,
There are 'Get up in the
morning' glories
In the Golden Afternoon…"

So, as the song went on, flower bells rang out and many other blossoms joined to form a wonderful orchestra.

"Come on, Alice!" cried the bread-and-butterflies, tugging at the little girl's skirt. "Come and join in." And Alice thoroughly enjoyed singing with a Pansy Choir.

"That was *lovely*!" she declared, when the music died away.

"Maybe," said Daisy, "but what flower are you?"

"Flower?" echoed the little girl. "I'm not a flower."

“Oh!” squealed Iris. “She isn’t a flower so she must be a weed. Daffodils! Quickly! Empty some water over her and drive her away. We don’t want weeds like *her* in our beds. Chase her away. Shoo!”

“But I’m not——” began Alice, when the Daffodils drenched her with water and she fled at top speed thinking that, if she were her right size, she would be able to pick all the flowers in a few minutes.

“A … E … I … O … Uuuuuuu!” sang a voice, as little Alice pushed through the grass.

"Who is that?" she exclaimed. She looked up. "Oh!" she cried. "Well I *never* did." And laughter bubbled up inside her as she saw a Caterpillar, seated on a mushroom, smoking a strange-shaped pipe called a hookah and finishing his odd song.

"*Who* are *you*?" asked the Caterpillar, as he unfolded his many arms and legs and took a deep pull at the hookah.

"Me?" giggled Alice. "Well, to tell the truth, sir, I hardly know. You see, I've changed so many times lately."

"Humph!" murmured the Caterpillar. "Exactically what is your problem?"

"To be precise, sir," answered the little girl, "I should like to be a little larger. Three inches is such a silly height to be. Don't you agree?"

"No!" stormed the Caterpillar, turning red with wrath. "I do *not* agree. I am exactically three inches high and I think it is a very sensible height. How dare you speak the way you have just spokenated." Clouds of smoke rose from the Caterpillar's pipe and, when it cleared away, Alice saw that the creature had vanished; only its clothes, shoes and gloves were left.

"However," said a nearby butterfly in the Caterpillar's voice, "I forgive you because you are so stupid. Here is some advice. Eat ONE side of it and you'll grow bigger, eat the other side and you'll become even smaller. Good-bye! "

"Wait!" cried poor Alice, as the butterfly fluttered away. "*What* are you talking about?"

"The MUSHROOM!" came the fading voice. "The MUSHROOM! Byeeeee!" And he was gone.

"Oh, dear," sighed the little girl as she broke off a piece of mushroom from one side and a piece from the other side. "I wish I knew which was which." Then she took a nibble of one piece, shot up like a serpent, to disturb a bird in its nest, nibbled at the other piece and shrank as rapidly as she had grown, quickly licked the first piece again and slowly managed to get herself back to her proper size.

"Thank goodness!" she sighed, putting the mushroom pieces in her pocket. "Now I shall be all right."

But she wasn't, you know, because she wandered into a wood that was filled with signs reading:

THIS WAY. YONDER. THAT WAY. UP. DOWN. TURN LEFT. NO, RIGHT.

"Bother, *bother*, BOTHER!" wailed poor Alice. "Now, *where* do you suppose I've got to *now*?"

"Lose something?" asked a voice from a tree.

Alice looked up to see a cat's grin just appearing.

"Well, yes," she admitted. "I think I've lost myself. Why—" she went on as the body of a cat appeared, "you're a CAT."

"Right first time," grinned the cat, as he vanished again. "I'm the Cheshire Cat. But, if it is of any interest to you, I can tell you that he went THAT way." The cat reappeared long enough to point through the trees. "The White Rabbit, I mean," he added. "And if you ask the Mad Hatter or the March Hare they'll tell you where he is."

"Thank you!" cried Alice, as she dashed away.

It wasn't more than three and three-quarter minutes later when the little girl reached the March Hare's queer thatched cottage, to see a very curious-looking person wearing a hat marked 10/6 pouring out tea by pouring it through one sleeve and out from the other.

The March Hare was with him at a long tea table and, as soon as the Mad Hatter saw Alice, he picked up another teapot with three spouts and filled up three cups at one and the same time.

"Thank you," said Alice, sitting down. "I could do with some tea." Instantly the strange pair advanced toward her.

"No room! No room!" cried the Mad Hatter.

"Not an inch of room!" agreed the March Hare.

"But I thought there was plenty of room," protested Alice. "This *is* a birthday party, isn't it? I heard you singing about birthdays when I arrived."

"No!" shouted the Mad Hatter. "This is *not* a birthday party. It is an UNbirthday party."

"Un..." began the little girl in bewilderment.

"Certainly," declared the March Hare. "Everyone has ONE birthday a year, so the other 364 days are all UNbirthdays. But don't argue; move up." And he pushed Alice into the next seat as they all moved up one. "Have some more tea."

"But I haven't had any yet," shrilled the little girl.

"Why not?" A teapot lid popped up and there was a dormouse looking at Alice. "Tea is good for you. Tee-hee!"

BANG! The lid came down again and the little girl was just wondering if she *had* really seen the Dormouse, when the Mad Hatter nudged her and handed her a beautiful birthday cake.

"Now," he said, "blow out the candle and make your wish come true."

Alice puffed out her cheeks and blew.

WHIZZZZ! Spluttering wildly, the candle sailed up like a rocket.

"Now," said the Hare, "let's have your story, my dear. Start at the beginning. No, begin at the start."

"Yes, and stop when you come to the end!" added the Mad Hatter. "That is *most* important. Most!"

The little girl sighed and, although she didn't think it would do much good, she told her story and was right in the middle of it when the Mad Hatter and March Hare jumped up and, pulling Alice to her feet, began to dance round and round her.

10/6

"Stop it!" shrilled the girl, as she sat down again. "I must finish. I was just telling you how I met the cat——"

At the word CAT the Dormouse popped out of the teapot in a terrible stew.

"Silly!" shouted the March Hare. "Fancy saying the word C-A-T." He and the Mad Hatter managed to quiet the poor Dormouse. "Next time you want to say—you know what—take care that you spell the word—what we've just said—or poor Dormouse will be frightfully upset."

Alice sighed. "I've finished my story now," she declared. "All *I* want is to find the White Rabbit. He—" She broke off as none other than the White

Rabbit came dashing up. "Why—" she cried, "here he *is*." She smiled at the creature she had chased for so long. "*Please* wait until I—" she began.

"Sorry!" The White Rabbit looked at his watch. "I've no time. No time at all. I must hurry. HURRY! I'm later than ever."

"Late?" The Mad Hatter grabbed the watch and looked at it. "*Of course* you're late. This is two days slow." He opened the case and peered inside. "I see what's wrong. This watch is full of wheels and screws." And he began to dig out the watch's works with a fork, filling up the case with butter, sugar, spoons and anything else he could find. "There you are!" he finished, pushing the watch back to the White Rabbit.

The Rabbit groaned. "My watch!" he wailed. "And it was an UNbirthday present, too."

"Well, in that case," chorused the Hare and the Hatter, as they grabbed the White Rabbit and threw him over a wall, "a very Merry Unbirthday to you."

Alice had had enough of such nonsense. "Oh, Mr. Rabbit," she called, "wait for me." And dashed after him. "That was the silliest tea party I've ever been to!" she declared, as she plunged straight into a place labeled TULGEY WOOD. "I'm going straight home, that's what *I'm* going to do. *Straight home*!"

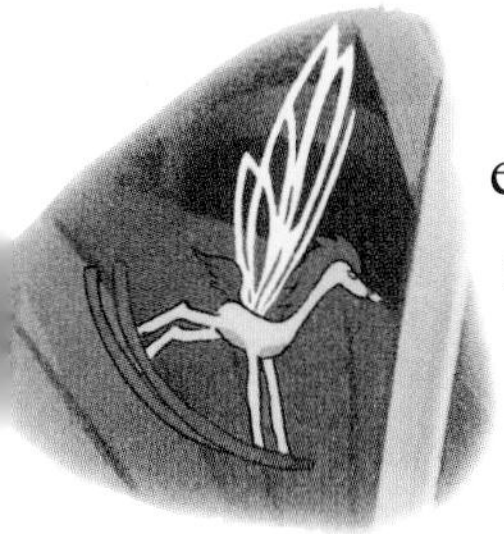

But the little girl found going straight home far from easy and if Alice hadn't met the Cheshire Cat again she might have been lost forever.

"Where were you bound for?" he asked.

"I'm going home!" cried Alice. "I'm finished with rabbits, blue, green, brown, pink or WHITE. All I want to do is to go home. Please tell me which way it is."

"The Queen's way," answered the Cat. "All ways here are the Queen's ways."

"But I haven't met any Queen," said Alice. She sniffed unhappily. "*Please* help me."

"Well," came the reply, "to find the Queen some go THIS way, some go THAT way and some go ANOTHER way but for me, myself, personally, I go THIS way!" The Cat pulled a lever to open a door in a tree. "Through there."

"Oh, thank you," cried the little girl, and she stepped through the door right into the Queen's garden. "I'll never forget you."

"Hee-hee!" laughed the Cat. "I'll make sure of THAT."

Inside the garden Alice found that the hedges on either side of the pathway had grown high and twisty and that she was, in fact, in a maze.

"We're painting the roses red," sang three voices. "We're painting the roses red."

"Who is and why are they?" murmured the little girl and, going through a gate she suddenly came upon—what *do* you suppose?— three Playing Cards busily splashing red paint on to white roses. "My goodness!" she exclaimed. "Why are you doing that?"

"Because, young person," answered the Cards in chorus, "we made a mistake in painting these roses white and the Queen likes them red. So, as we don't want to lose our heads, we're painting the roses—red, red roses—RED!"

"Can I help?" asked Alice.

"I don't know," laughed a Card. "Can you?"

"I'll try," said the little girl.

Alice was busily slapping on red paint when lots of things happened. There was a fanfare of trumpets, the White Rabbit appeared and blew his trumpet, the three Cards lined up and the Rabbit stuck out his chest and announced the arrival of the Queen's Card Guard. Up came dozens of Card Soldiers and, as they formed themselves into straight lines, the White Rabbit blew his trumpet again, stuck his chest out a lot more and cried in a voice that rang like a bell:

"Her IM-perial Highness, Her Excellency, Her Royal Majesty, Her Stupendosity, Her Mightiness, THE QUEEN OF HEARTS!"

The Queen stepped forward and a little King tapped the White Rabbit on the arm.

"And the King!" he whispered in a meek voice.

"*And* the King, of course!" cried the White Rabbit.

The Queen saw the dripping rose trees.

"Who has been painting my roses RED?" she shouted. Then she saw the three drooping Cards. "You, eh! Right! Off with their heads. Off with them. *Off!* OFF!"

"Oh, oh, please," pleaded Alice. "They were only trying to please."

"Who is *this*?" stormed the Queen.

Alice tried her best to explain that she was not a Heart, a Club, a Diamond or a Spade, but just a little girl trying to find her way home.

"Humph!" muttered Her Royal Mightiness. "I suppose you know that all ways are MY ways?"

"Y-yes, Your IM-perial Greatness," stammered Alice. "I——"

"Don't talk," thundered the Queen. "Do you play croquet? It's a game played with mallets, balls and hoops."

"Yes, Your Wondrosity!" said Alice.

"Good!" snapped the Queen. "Then, let the game begin."

"Tra-la-la-la-toot-TOOT!" The White Rabbit blew on his trumpet, the Cards scattered, someone produced a hedgehog for a ball, someone else brought forward a number of long-necked birds called flamingoes, who were to act as mallets, and the strangest game of croquet Alice had ever played, started.

"*Weeek!*" went the little girl's flamingo, just as the Queen was about to hit the hedgehog-ball.

"Silence!" she screamed. Then she swung her strange mallet, missed, hacked a lump out of the grass and was so cross that the King quickly made the hedgehog-ball scamper through a hoop made by a Card. "Ah!" cried the Queen. "A good shot, I think. Now it is your turn, my dear!" And she almost smiled upon Alice.

Then came trouble, because Alice's flamingo misbehaved itself. It twisted itself in such a way that the player was in the mallet's position and the mallet in the player's position. At last the little girl *did* manage to hit the ball, however, and, turning, she almost fainted when she saw first the Cheshire Cat's tail, and then the whole broadly grinning Cat sitting cheekily on the Queen's bustle—which was a bunched-up portion of her dress right behind her.

"Hello!" said the Cat. "I told you you'd not be allowed to forget me. How are you getting on?"

"Not very well, I'm afraid," answered Alice.

"Who are you talking to?" snapped the Queen.

"The—the Cheshire Cat, Your Royal Highness!" she answered.

"Cat?" screamed the Queen. "I see no Cat. I warn you, child, I might soon lose my temper. Yes, I *am* losing my temper. THERE! I've lost it. No! Not quite!" She scowled at Alice. "Much more of this, however, and I shall lose my temper and you will lose your head."

"Hee-hee!" laughed the Cat. "We could easily make her really angry. Shall we try? It would be *such* fun."

"Oh, no! No, no!" wailed Alice, as she saw the mischievous Cat seize the Queen's flamingo and cause Her IM-perial Majesty to fall over. "Stop it, Cheshire Cat. Please stop it!"

But it was too late. Up rose the Queen and glared round her. "That

has finished it," she screamed. "Now I *have* lost my temper and YOU—" she pointed at Alice, "*you* shall lose your head."

Suddenly the King tugged at his wife's dress.

"Yes, Alphonse, what *is* it?" snapped the Queen irritably.

"Ah—er—umn!" began the little King. "It's just this, my dear. We *must* have a trial first. Only a teeny-weeny little trial, of course, but don't you think we ought to have *something* of the kind. It might be fun!" he added.

The Queen looked at her King, then at Alice and finally at the King again.

"Yes," she agreed, "perhaps you are right. Very well, then, LET THE TRIAL BEGIN."

After that the little girl hardly knew what was happening. The Card soldiers swooped down upon her, she was whisked up and away and in next to no time at all she found herself in a courtroom and, what was worse, in the prisoner's dock.

"Tra-la-la-toot-toot!"

The White Rabbit blew his trumpet and announced:

"Your Majesties, Members of the Jury, Loyal Subjects—"

The little King waddled forward and tapped his arm.

"—and the King!" finished the Rabbit. "The trial of Alice is about to begin."

"Very well," said the Queen, glaring at the prisoner. "Are you ready for your sentence?"

"But what about a verdict first?" pleaded Alice.

"Sentence first, verdict afterward," the Queen thundered, "but just to make things different we will call some witnesses. Has anyone any witnesses?"

As it happened there were any number of witnesses and the first was March Hare, who was carried into court by his ears in the grasp of two Card Guards.

"What do YOU know of this horrible crime?" asked the Queen. "I know nothing!" came the Hare's reply.

"Ah!" murmured the Royal Lady. "That is important. *Most* important. Call the next witness."

This proved to be the Mad Hatter, who immediately presented the Queen with an UNbirthday cake.

"How splendid!" cried Her Royal Somebody. "Shall I blow out the candles on it?" And, before the Hatter could answer, she puffed out her cheeks and blew a great blow.

BANG!

Up went the cake and down it came again in hundreds of pieces. While all this was going on, Alice put her hands into her apron pockets and found the pieces of mushroom. She quickly put them into her mouth and instantly she began to grow and grow and *grow* and GROW until she towered over everybody.

"Poof!" shouted Alice, almost the only one who was not afraid. "I'm not scared of you. You're not a Queen at all. You're just a fat, pompous, bad-tempered——" She paused and looked around. She was beginning to shrink and when she was quite small again she finished her sentence in a tiny voice… "tyrant!"

"*What* did you say, my dear?" cooed the Queen, with a very unpleasant smile.

"Why, simply that you were a pompous, fat, bad-tempered old tyrant!" laughed the mischievous Cheshire Cat, as he perched on the Queen's crown.

"WHAT?" roared the Royal Personage. "OFF WITH HER HEAD."

At once the Card Guards rushed at Alice from all sides, but she pushed them off and raced into the garden.

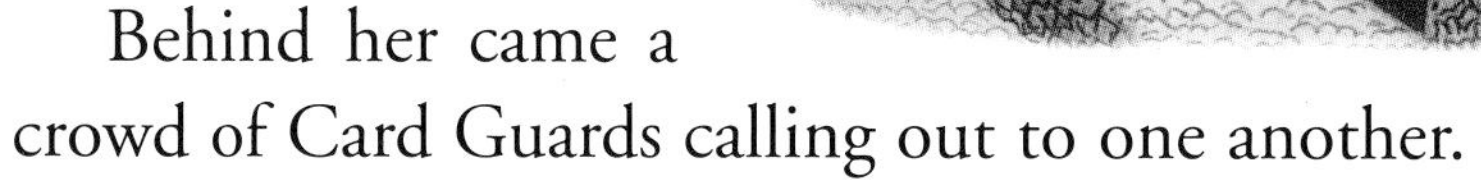

"Off with her head!" the King was shouting, as he used his crown as a kind of trumpet. "Off with it."

"It was all the fault of that wicked Cat," sobbed the little girl as she ran, criss-cross, higgledy-piggledy, through a maze of pathways. "I never *did* like him. Never!"

Behind her came a crowd of Card Guards calling out to one another.

"Which way?"

"This way!?

"That way!"

"No, the other way!"

Suddenly everything went quite, quite mad. If things had been strange before, what with White Rabbits with watches, a Dodo riding on a Toucan's beak, a March Hare having an UNbirthday, a Walrus eating oysters, cakes that made one grow big and other things that made one small, flowers that talked and goodness *knows* what else, now things were quite, quite mad.

In a flash Alice ran out of the garden and on to a beach. The girl hopped over rocks until they turned into teapots and the beach was a tabletop.

"Got her!" cried a familiar voice, and the March Hare grabbed at Alice.

"Have a cup of tea, my dear?" begged the Mad Hatter. "We've just made twenty-six fresh pots and there's plenty of pepper to make them hot. Please stay!"

"No!" screamed Alice as she struggled.

SPLASH!

They all three fell into a giant cup of tea, and as the little girl swam she saw the Caterpillar, still puffing away at his hookah pipe.

"Oh, Mister Caterpillar," she cried, "what shall I do?"

"*Who* are *you*?" snapped the creature, as he blew a big smoke ring that swirled itself into a long tunnel.

Down the tunnel rushed poor Alice until she came to a door.

"Still locked, my dear," said the Doorknob, "but why go *inside* when you are already outside? Look and see!"

Puzzled, Alice peered through the keyhole. “Why,” she exclaimed, “that *is* me outside. I’m asleep. Hurrah!”

"Alice!" came her sister's voice. "Alice! Pay attention and tell me what I have been reading about?"

The little girl blinked in the strong sunlight and rubbed her eyes. "I—er—I c-can't remember," she whispered, "but I've had such a strange adventure. There was a White Rabbit who had a watch and was in a terrible hurry. Then I fell down a well and..."

"Oh, for goodness' sake, Alice," cried her elder sister. "Do stop talking such nonsense. Come along. It's time for tea. You *are* a strange child."

Alice smiled to herself as she got up and went along with her sister, and she murmured under her breath: "Not nearly so strange as *some* people!"